THIS LITTLE TIGER BOOK BELONGS TO:

_____

_____

_____

_____

For Doris and George
– A.H.B.

For Matthew and Sally
– J.C.

This edition published 1997
First published in the United States 1996 by Little Tiger Press,
12221 West Feerick Street, Wauwatosa, WI 53222
Originally published in Great Britain 1996 by Magi Publications, London
Text © 1996 A.H. Benjamin
Illustrations © 1996 Jane Chapman
Library of Congress Cataloging-in-Publication Data
Benjamin, A. H. . 1950–
What if? / by A.H. Benjamin ; pictures by Jane Chapman.   p.   cm.
Summary : Although none of them have seen the kangaroo that has just arrived
at Buttercup Farm, all the animals worry that she might take over their jobs.
ISBN 1-888444-14-2 (pb)   [1. Domestic animals—Fiction.   2. Kangaroos—Fiction.]
I. Chapman, Jane, 1970- ill. II. Title.
PZ7. B43457Wh 1996 [E]–dc20 96-14618 CIP AC
Printed and bound in Hong Kong
First U.S. paperback edition
1 3 5 7 9 10 8 6 4 2

What if?

by A.H.Benjamin

Pictures by Jane Chapman

Little Tiger Press

Something special was happening on Buttercup Farm. The farmer had bought a kangaroo, and it was arriving that very day! The farmyard animals had never seen a kangaroo before.

"What can a kangaroo do,
anyway?" they wondered.
But nobody knew.

"What if she can crow?" said Rooster. "What if she gets up very early every morning and crows so loudly that she wakes up the whole farm? Perhaps she would even count the hens and chicks to see if any are missing. Then the farmer wouldn't need me anymore, and I'd have to look for another job. *Cock-a-doodle-doo!* I might not find one!"

"How dreadful!"

said everyone.

"What if she can herd sheep?" said Dog. "What if she rounds them all up and takes them to graze on the highest and greenest hills? She might even chase a fox or two. The farmer would be so pleased with her that he'd send me to live in the kennels. *Woof!* I would hate that!"

"How horrible!"

said everyone.

"What if she can catch mice?" said Cat.
"What if she catches all the mice in the
barn and a few rats, too? Maybe even
the spiders would be scared to live there.
Then the farmer would get rid of me,
and I would become a stray.
Meow! I'd miss my milk
and sardines!"

"How awful!"

said everyone.

"What if she can give milk?" said Cow. "What if she fills up all the pails on the farm with such rich, creamy milk that everybody wants to buy it? Then nobody would want mine, and the farmer would make me pull the plow instead. *Moo!* I'd miss my cozy stall!"

"How appalling!"

said everyone.

"What if she can grow wool?" said Sheep.
"What if she has a thick, woolly fleece that
is whiter than snow and softer than silk?
And maybe her coat will grow twice as
fast as mine. The farmer would be so
delighted that he'd only use *my* wool
to stuff old pillows and cushions.
Baa! I couldn't stand that!"

"How terrible!"
said everyone.

"What if she can pull a cart?" said Horse.
"What if she can take a cartful of fruit and
vegetables to the market faster than I can?
She might even give rides to the farmer's two
children. Then there would be no place for me,
and I would end up in an old horses' home.
Neigh! I'd miss all my friends here!"

"How frightful!"

said everyone.

They were so busy worrying they
didn't notice that some of the young
farm animals were missing.
"Where are my puppies?" asked Dog.

"And my kittens?" asked Cat.
"And my lamb?" asked Sheep.

All the animals searched
and searched, but they could
not find a kitten, nor a puppy,
nor a tiny lamb anywhere.
They looked from the barn . . .

. . . to the pigsty, with no luck.
"This is dreadful!" crowed Rooster.
"Horrible!" woofed Dog.
"Awful!" meowed Cat.

"Appalling!" mooed Cow.
"Terrible!" baaed Sheep.
"Frightful!" neighed Horse.
Suddenly, across the field they saw . . .

. . . a very strange animal,
leaping and bounding
toward them.

"Hello," it said.
"I'm Kangaroo!"

The animals couldn't
believe their eyes.
Kangaroo had a big
pouch in her tummy,
and in the pouch . . .

... were
three kittens,
two puppies
and
one tiny lamb!

"We've had so much fun going on a tour of the farm," said Kangaroo. "What if I were to be their baby-sitter every day!" "*What a good idea!*" the animals cried. And with crowing, barking, meowing, mooing, baaing and neighing, they all welcomed Kangaroo to her new home.

Some more books from
LITTLE TIGER PRESS
for you to enjoy

ROBBIE RABBIT AND THE LITTLE ONES
by Julie Sykes and pictures by Catherine Walters
ISBN 1-888444-11-8 $4.95
When Robbie Rabbit plays hide-and-seek with his little brothers and sisters
he can't find them anywhere—but he does find something far more scary!
"An endearing story which children will love to hear and later read"
—*Children's Book Review Service*

I DON'T WANT TO GO TO BED!
by Julie Sykes and pictures by Tim Warnes
ISBN 1-888444-13-4 $5.95
Little Tiger does not like going to bed. But when he happily runs off one
night he finds himself alone and lost in the dark jungle . . .
"A charming and satisfying twist to a timeless dilemma of childhood, this
wonderful story and colorful, happy illustrations are certain to be a hit."
—*Kendal Rautzhan, Books to Borrow . . . Books to Buy*

LAZY OZZIE
by Michael Coleman and pictures by Gwyneth Williamson
ISBN 1-888444-12-6 $4.95
Ozzie is too lazy to learn how to fly, and he thinks up a clever plan to make
his mother believe that he can—but is she really fooled?
"Skillful watercolor and ink illustrations add bounce, but never get in the way
of the story."—*Kirkus Reviews*

LITTLE TIGER PRESS
12221 West Feerick Street, Wauwatosa, WI 53222